JF
Krulik, Nancy E.
Rulin' the school

D0723974

"Salem Saberhagen, you are accused of making phony phone calls," Judge Gree declared.

"Your honor, how did you know the caller was my client?" Salem's lawyer asked.

The judge gave Salem a triumphant grin. "Ever hear of caller ID, Mr. Saberhagen?" she demanded. "I had the phone number of the caller all the time."

Salem sighed and shrunk down in his seat. Now he knew where he had heard Judge Gree's voice before. She was the woman he had woken up to ask about her refrigerator.

Oh man! Salem thought miserably. *I can't believe I called a member of the Witches' Council.*

"Salem Saberhagen, I hereby sentence you to a term of three weeks at the Other Realm Obedience Boarding School. Maybe there you will learn how to behave!"

This is going to be a breeze, Salem thought smugly.

Of course, Salem had been wrong before.

WITHDRAWN FROM THE RECORDS OF THE
MID-CONTINENT PUBLIC LIBRARY

MID-CONTINENT PUBLIC LIBRARY
Antioch Branch
6060 N. Chestnut Ave.
Gladstone, Mo. 64119
AN

Sabrina, the Teenage Witch™
Salem's Tails™

Available from MINSTREL Books

For orders other than by individual consumers, Pocket Books grants a discount on the purchase of **10 or more** copies of single titles for special markets or premium use. For further details, please write to the Vice President of Special Markets, Pocket Books, 1230 Avenue of the Americas, 9th Floor, New York, NY 10020-1586.

For information on how individual consumers can place orders, please write to Mail Order Department, Simon & Schuster Inc., 100 Front Street, Riverside, NJ 08075.

Sabrina
The Teenage Witch

Salem's Tails ®

RULIN' THE SCHOOL

Nancy Krulik

Based upon the characters in Archie Comics

**And based upon the television series
Sabrina, The Teenage Witch
Created for television by Nell Scovell
Developed for television by Jonathan Schmock**

Illustrated by Mark Dubowski

A MINSTREL® BOOK

Published by POCKET BOOKS
New York   London   Toronto   Sydney   Singapore

The sale of this book without its cover is unauthorized. If you purchased this book without a cover, you should be aware that it was reported to the publisher as "unsold and destroyed." Neither the author nor the publisher has received payment for the sale of this "stripped book."

This book is a work of fiction. Names, characters, places and incidents are products of the author's imagination or are used fictitiously. Any resemblance to actual events or locales or persons living or dead is entirely coincidental.

A MINSTREL PAPERBACK *Original*

A Minstrel Book published by
POCKET BOOKS, a division of Simon & Schuster Inc.
1230 Avenue of the Americas, New York, NY 10020

Copyright © 2000 by Viacom Productions, Inc. All rights reserved.

Salem Quotes taken from the following episodes:
"The Big Sleep" written by Sheldon Bull
"Salem & Juliette" written by Carrie Honigblum & Renee Phillips

All rights reserved, including the right to reproduce this book or portions thereof in any form whatsoever. For information address Pocket Books, 1230 Avenue of the Americas, New York, NY 10020

ISBN: 0-671-03835-4

First Minstrel Books printing May 2000

10 9 8 7 6 5 4 3 2 1

A MINSTREL BOOK and colophon are registered trademarks of Simon & Schuster Inc.

SABRINA THE TEENAGE WITCH and all related titles, logos and characters are trademarks of Archie Comics Publications, Inc.

Cover photo by Pat Hill Studio

Printed in the U.S.A.

MID-CONTINENT PUBLIC LIBRARY

3 0001 00543246 5

MID-CONTINENT PUBLIC LIBRARY
Antioch Branch
6060 N. Chestnut Ave.
Gladstone, Mo. 64119

AN

For Amanda and Ian,
who totally rule their school!

"Thanks, but I can defend myself. I'm not the high school nerd I used to be. . . . Okay, I'm done being brave. Sabrina!"

—*Salem*

Chapter 1

"Aaaaaahhhhh!"

Hilda Spellman opened the door to her freezer and let out a loud, frightening scream. Her sister Zelda raced into the kitchen to see what the matter was.

"Hilda, what's wrong?" Zelda asked.

Hilda didn't answer. She opened her mouth wide, but nothing came out. So instead, she pointed to the inside of the freezer.

Zelda peeked her head inside. There,

1

in the corner, she saw a large, gray rat. Quickly, Zelda reached her hand into the freezer and bravely pulled the animal out by its tail.

"You were afraid of *this*?" Zelda asked her sister as she dangled the lifeless rat in front of her.

Hilda nodded and moved back nervously.

"But it's only a *rubber* rat. It's not real."

Suddenly Hilda found her voice. "Salem!" she shouted. "I'll get you for this."

Salem, the Spellman's black cat, didn't move from his hiding place under the kitchen table. "*Moi?*" he asked in an all-too-innocent voice. "Why would you be angry at *me*?"

Hilda pointed her finger toward Salem. Instantly the kitchen table rose up high in the air—revealing the cat who was hiding beneath it. Salem shivered nervously.

Now there was nothing standing between him and one *very* angry witch.

"Are you trying to tell me that you weren't the one who put that fake rat in the freezer?" Hilda demanded.

Salem didn't deny it. He simply looked up at Hilda and scowled (well, as much as you can scowl when you don't really have any lips). "Why do you always accuse *me* of doing things? Other people live in this house, too." He stared at Zelda.

"Me?" Zelda declared. "I would *never* do such a thing."

"Give me a break, Salem," Hilda agreed. "Zelda's not exactly known for her jokes."

Zelda raised an eyebrow at her sister.

Salem shrugged his little furry shoulders. "Well, what about Sabrina then? She's a *teenager*. You know how weird teenagers can be."

3

Before Hilda and Zelda could even consider that possibility, Sabrina came bursting into the kitchen. Her face was beet red, and her eyes were almost bulging out of her head. She wore a bright pink bandana across her forehead.

"Let me at him! I'll strangle that cat!" Sabrina demanded. Salem ducked under a chair, but not fast enough to avoid Sabrina's eyes. She was so angry, she didn't even notice that her Aunt Zelda was dangling a large rubber rat by its tail or that the kitchen table was now flying in the air.

Zelda jumped between her niece and the family cat.

"Why are you angry with Salem?" Zelda asked calmly.

Sabrina whipped the bandana off of her head and pointed to a big black circle in the middle of her forehead. "This is why. Salem tricked me into going to school with this circle on my forehead. And today was picture day. I didn't find out the circle was there until *after* my photo was taken. I'm going to look like this in the yearbook!"

Zelda seemed confused. "How did he trick you into putting a circle on your head?"

"At breakfast this morning he bet me that I couldn't make a quarter stick to my forehead. And I bet him that I could. I was wrong. And to make matters worse, I didn't know that he had used a pencil to color a dark line all around the quarter. The pencil left a circle on my face. I can't believe the photographer didn't mention it to me before he took my picture!"

"He probably thought it was some new teenage fad or something," Sabrina's aunt Hilda suggested.

Sabrina glared at her.

5

Salem started laughing from his hiding place beneath the chair. "I wondered when you'd get a-*round* to figuring it out!"

Sabrina leaped toward Salem, but her aunts stopped her. "I was so embarrassed, I just left school and popped right home. I don't know how I'll ever be able to go back."

Zelda smiled at her. "It's easy—just walk straight for three blocks and make a left at the light."

Sabrina was shocked. "You don't mean you're going to make me go back after I was so embarrassed?"

Zelda nodded. "That's exactly what I mean. I'm sure everyone has forgotten all about this by now. And you can retake the yearbook picture later this month— they always let you do that. Besides, I have a dinner date with Willard Kraft tonight, and I don't want to have to spend the whole time talking about how you missed school today."

Willard Kraft was Zelda's boyfriend—and Sabrina's principal at school. The idea of her aunt having a romantic meal with her principal gave Sabrina the creeps.

"Could this day get any worse?" she muttered as she went over to the kitchen sink and started scrubbing away the mark on her forehead. "If I were you, Salem, I'd sleep with one eye open tonight! Remember, *I* have powers and you don't!" And just to prove it, Sabrina pointed her finger toward Salem's food bowl. *Poof!* The food disappeared instantly.

"Hey!" Salem complained. "That was canned salmon—one of my favorites!"

Salem was a little nervous now. Sabrina was right—he was the only one in the Spellman household who did not have magic powers. Of course, it hadn't always been that way. Once Salem had been a

7

warlock. But he'd used his magic to try to take over the world. For that, the Witches' Council had sentenced him to one hundred years as a cat. Later, they'd added fifty years to his sentence for bad behavior.

Now, here he was, the once-powerful Salem Saberhagen, living as a cat in a house of witches. Or, as Salem preferred to refer to himself, a *familiar* living in a house of witches. Witches and warlocks who had been turned into other creatures were often called familiars. Salem thought "familiar" sounded much more sophisticated than "cat."

To make matters worse, the Spellmans didn't even live in a fancy mansion in some exotic locale like the Pleasure Dome. Sabrina and her aunts lived in an old house in a small Massachusetts town. And it wasn't even a house that was a stop on the local garden club tour! Life at the Spellman house was just plain boring for Salem. That's why he played pranks on people. It livened things up.

"Salem, you have to stop this practical joking," Zelda scolded the cat as Sabrina left the house. "It's going to get you into trouble one day."

Chapter 2

That night, at five minutes to seven, Sabrina raced for the door. She wanted to get out of the house before she had to spend one extra minute with Mr. Kraft, and he was due to arrive any second. Sabrina really hated the principal. Once, for her Aunt Zelda's sake, Sabrina had tried to look for one small thing that she could like about Mr. Kraft. But she'd come up empty. There wasn't anything likable about him at all.

Sabrina wasn't surprised to hear Aunt Hilda's footsteps barreling down the stairs behind her. Hilda hated Willard Kraft almost as much as Sabrina did. At one time, Willard had had a crush on Hilda. Hilda was still certain that Willard was only dating Zelda to get to her. Sabrina's aunts argued about that all the time.

Zelda beat them both to the door. "Just where do you two think you're going?" Zelda asked her niece and her sister as she blocked their paths.

"We're um . . . er . . . well . . ." Sabrina stammered and looked anxiously to her aunt Hilda for help.

Hilda thought quickly, pointed her finger, and zapped two black shiny vacuum cleaners onto the floor beside Sabrina. "We're going for a little spin in the sky," she told her sister. "That's why we've got our flying vacuums all gassed up and ready to go."

11

"On a school night? And before Sabrina does her homework?"

"I'm, uh, studying for my astronomy test," Sabrina lied.

"Good one," Aunt Hilda whispered in Sabrina's ear. She smiled at her sister. "Well, gotta go. See ya!"

Sabrina and Aunt Hilda grabbed their vacuums and got ready to go.

Unfortunately, as soon as Sabrina opened the door, Willard Kraft walked up onto the porch. Sabrina rolled her eyes. She hated seeing the principal after school. Come to think of it, she didn't like seeing him *in* school very much, either.

"Hello Sabrina," Mr. Kraft said in his stuffy voice.

"Hello," Sabrina replied. "Goodbye."

And with that, Sabrina and Hilda went outside into the night.

"Why were they bringing vacuum

cleaners outside with them?" Willard asked Zelda as she invited him in.

"They are going to a Dust Bunnies Busters meeting. Their mission is to wipe out dust and dinginess throughout the world," Zelda lied. She knew she couldn't tell Willard that Hilda and Sabrina were off for a late-night flight. No human was allowed to know that the Spellmans were a family of witches. If a human found out and told someone else their secret, they would all lose their powers.

"I had no idea Sabrina was such a neat freak. You'd never know it from her locker," Willard mused.

"Would you like something to drink?" Zelda asked, as she tried to change the subject.

"Seltzer would be fine," Mr. Kraft replied.

"I'll be right back," Zelda said with a smile. Quickly she raced into the kitchen,

filled two glasses with soda water and ice cubes, and ran back to Willard.

Zelda sat down on the couch beside Willard and looked into his eyes. Willard's face twisted into an expression that sort of resembled a smile.

"Zelda . . ." he began. "I really lo . . ."

But before Willard Kraft could finish his sentence, he glanced into his glass and let out a shriek. Then he jumped up on the couch and screamed, pointing to his glass.

Zelda couldn't imagine what was going on. In a house full of witches, people were always popping in and out. Had someone from her family popped into Willard's drink?

Luckily, that wasn't it at all.

"There's a spider in there!" Willard exclaimed finally.

Zelda looked in the glass. Sure enough, there was a small black spider inside one of the ice cubes. She reached in with her finger and fished out the cube. Then she shook it off and examined it. The cube was made of plastic, not frozen water. And the spider inside the plastic ice cube was made of rubber. It wouldn't hurt a fly (or any other insect for that matter).

"Oh for heaven sake," she laughed. "It's a rubber spider."

Willard didn't care. "I hate *any* kind of spider!"

Zelda smiled. "Why Willard, you're arachnophobic," she said, using the big scientific word for someone who is afraid of spiders. Zelda always used big, scientific words. "I never knew that about you. That's so cute."

"Maybe I am afraid of spiders," Willard said, as he nervously wiped the beads of sweat from his moustache, straightened out his tie, and readjusted his wire-framed

15

glasses. "But everyone's afraid of something. Just get that thing away from me." Quickly, he grabbed his hat and coat and bolted straight for the front door.

"Willard, wait. You were just about to say something," Zelda urged, hoping that he was going to tell her something romantic.

"I think I'd better be going."

Just then, Zelda heard a familiar deep-sounding chuckle coming from the kitchen.

As Willard opened the door, Zelda roared, *"Salem!* I'm going to get you for this!"

Willard stopped at the porch steps and looked curiously at Zelda. "Why are you yelling at the cat?"

Zelda had no answer for him. Even if she could tell Willard the truth, he'd never believe her!

Chapter 3

Salem was really depressed. It had been two weeks since he'd pulled the practical jokes on Sabrina and her aunts, and they were still mad at him. Hilda was feeding him bargain-brand cat food. Zelda had taken away his TV privileges. And Sabrina kept using her finger to magically move his water bowl every time he tried to take a drink. Usually that meant that Salem would fall face first into the bowl. And if there was one thing

17

Salem really hated, it was cold water on his fur.

But right now, Zelda, Hilda, and Sabrina had all gone to some sort of witch meeting. Salem was alone in the house. So it was time for a little fun. First, he went into the kitchen and loosened the top on the sugar shaker.

I can't wait to see Hilda's face when she tries to add a little sugar to her coffee, Salem thought mischievously.

Then the short-haired black cat padded his way up the stairs to Sabrina's room. At first he looked around for a trick he could play on Sabrina. But then he reconsidered. Pulling a gag on Hilda was one thing—she was mature enough to get angry without actually harming Salem (well, usually, anyway). Sabrina didn't have quite so much self-control. Maybe it was better to let up on her for a while.

Salem's eyes fell on Sabrina's speakerphone. "Perfect!" he declared as he walked over to the desk and opened Sabrina's Other Realm Phone Book.

Salem closed his eyes, and let his paw land on one of the names on page 433. Then he opened his eyes, and looked at the number he had pointed to: 555–8796. Salem used his paw to dial. The phone rang once.

"Hello?" the voice on the other end said.

"Hello," Salem replied in a very deep voice. "I am a representative of the Malata Snew Company. And we'd like to offer you a free box of snew, just for agreeing to take a small survey."

"What's snew?" the person asked Salem.

Salem started to laugh. "Nothin' much. What's new with you?"

As Salem used his paw to quickly hang up the speakerphone, he roared with laughter. *There's nothing like a phony*

phone call to brighten your day, he thought.

Salem turned to another page of the Other Realm Phone Book. Once again he closed his eyes and pointed to a phone number. Then he opened his eyes and began dialing the new number: he dialed 555–3785.

The phone rang several times before a woman's sleepy voice finally picked up. "Hello?"

"Hello," Salem replied, using a high-pitched voice this time. "I'm calling from the O.R. Electric Company, and we're taking a survey. We'd like you to answer a few simple questions."

"Okay, sure."

"Is your refrigerator running?" Salem asked.

"Yes it is," the sleepy woman replied.

Salem couldn't control himself. He started chuckling even before he gave the punch line. "Then you'd better go and catch it!" he blurted out just before he used his paw to turn off the phone.

Then Salem tried another number. This time, when the person on the other end picked up the phone, it was Salem who said "Hello?" first.

"Hello?" the person on the other end replied.

"Hello?" Salem asked again.

"Who is this?" the person demanded.

"Who is this?" Salem answered.

"You called me."

"No I didn't, you called me," Salem said.

"No, I didn't."

"Sure you did. I don't even know who you are. Why would I call you?" Salem asked.

By this time, the person on the other end was totally confused. And that made Salem laugh. Once he did that, the joke was over. So he used his paw to turn off

21

the phone, and got ready to pull his next telephone gag.

Salem was having so much fun making the calls, that he decided to spend the rest of the day picking numbers from the phone book and playing jokes on perfect strangers. He was so busy, he didn't hear the door to the linen closet open and shut, twice.

These are the ultimate practical jokes, he thought after making one particularly funny call. *These people can't get back at me, because they don't know who I am.*

Just then Zelda appeared at Sabrina's bedroom door—accompanied by two armed guards from the Other Realm.

"Salem Saberhagen, you are under arrest for making phony phone calls," one of the guards told him. "You have been summoned to appear before a Witches' Council court in the Other Realm."

Salem gulped. *Then again, maybe they can.*

Chapter 4

Before Salem even knew what was happening, he found himself in a giant courtroom in the Other Realm. Zelda, Sabrina, and Hilda had been banned from the proceedings. Salem had never felt so alone.

He looked around the courtroom for a friendly face. But everyone looked stern and angry. Suddenly, the back door of the courtroom swung open. In walked a warlock, who looked to be about twenty-five years old. He was wearing a brown suit that had a tear in the back of the pants. His tie was crooked, his eyeglasses were taped together at the nose, and his shoes were untied. His bright red hair was standing on end—as though he'd forgotten to brush it that morning. Just as he reached the table where Salem sat, the warlock tripped over his shoelace, and dropped a pile of folders all over the floor.

"Oops. Sorry," he apologized as he struggled to put all the papers back in their proper place. He reached out a hand to Salem. Salem looked at him curiously. How was Salem supposed to shake hands with this character? Salem didn't even *have* hands!

The warlock must have realized his mistake, because he shyly put his hand to the side and stood up. "Hello," he said.

"I'm your court-appointed lawyer, Benny Frank."

Salem moaned. This was terrible.

"Now I know you might be a little nervous because this is my first case," Benny began.

"Well, I wasn't nervous until you *told* me this was your first case," Salem hissed.

"Oh. Well, anyway, you don't have to be worried. This is an open and shut case that we're sure to win, Mr. uh . . ." Benny looked at a sheet of paper. "Mr. McConnell."

"I'm not Mr. McConnell," Salem said.

"Well, I know. *Now* you're a cat. But when you were a warlock, you were . . ."

Salem shook his little furry head furiously. "I was never Mr. McConnell. I'm Salem Saberhagen."

Benny dug through his pile of folders until he came to one marked "Saber-

hagen." He opened the file and looked at the pages inside.

"Oh. In that case, I guess you *do* have something to be worried about," Benny told Salem.

Salem groaned.

Just then the bailiff came into the courtroom. "All rise for the Honorable Judge Ann Gree," he said.

"Ann Gree," Salem repeated. "That sounds a lot like *angry*. That can't be good."

Benny nodded. "I told you."

Salem rested his head in his paws.

"Be seated," Judge Gree told the court.

Salem's ears perked up. He knew that voice from somewhere. Of course the last time he'd heard it, it sounded a little more tired. But it was definitely the same voice. Now where had Salem heard Judge Ann Gree's voice before?

"Salem Saberhagen, you are accused

of making phony phone calls. I will not even bother to ask you how you plead, because I know for a fact that you are guilty!"

"Aren't you going to object to that?" Salem hissed at Benny.

"Well, I mean, if she says that you're guilty, then . . ."

Salem bared his claws.

"Oh all right," Benny agreed. "I object. How do you know that, your honor?"

"Because he made one of those calls to my house! Objection overruled."

Benny looked at Salem and shrugged helplessly.

"Ask her how she knew it was me," Salem replied.

"Oooh. Good question. I wish I'd thought of it," Benny complimented Salem. "Your honor, how did you know the caller was my client?"

The judge gave Salem a triumphant

grin. "Ever hear of caller ID, Mr. Saberhagen?" she demanded. "I had the phone number of the caller all the time. And since Hilda, Zelda, and Sabrina Spellman were all at a meeting here in the Other Realm, that only leaves you."

Salem sighed and shrunk down in his seat. Now he knew where he had heard Judge Gree's voice before. She was the woman he had woken up to ask about her refrigerator.

Oh man! Salem thought miserably. *I can't believe I called a member of the Witches' Council.*

Salem leaped out of his chair and landed right on the judge's lap. He looked up, batted his eyes at the judge, and purred. "I throw myself at the mercy of the court," he declared.

"Aaachoo!" Judge Gree sneezed. "Get off of me! I'm allergic to familiars—especially cats! Aachoo!"

Salem slid off her lap and slinked back to his seat. "Sorry," he said slowly.

Salem's stomach was beginning to churn. He was already sentenced to 150 years as a cat. What if Judge Ann Gree added more time to that sentence? How much longer could Salem survive on a diet of kibbles and kidneys without going crazy?

"Salem Saberhagen, I hereby sentence you to a term of three weeks at the Other Realm Obedience Boarding School. Maybe there you will learn how to behave!"

And with that, the judge stood and left to courtroom.

Salem smiled to himself. Boarding school. How bad could that be? Salem had been to school once before—when he was a young warlock. And he'd been very successful there. He'd even suc-ceeded in taking over the entire student council—until the principal managed to free himself from the bottle Salem had trapped him in.

This is going to be a breeze, Salem thought smugly.

Of course, Salem had been wrong before.

Chapter 5

Salem wasn't even allowed to go home and pack before going off to obedience school. He was taken directly from the court to the school. And that meant he was going to have to spend three whole weeks without his soft fluffy cat pillow, his private stash of canned chunky white tuna, and his bubble bath. After all, this was a boarding school. Salem would have to sleep here. And he couldn't go home for his supplies.

31

As if that wasn't bad enough, he was taken to the school in a pet carrier. (Now for most cats, that would have seemed perfectly normal, but even after years as a familiar Salem had trouble thinking of himself as a cat.)

Once he was inside the school, Salem was free to walk on his own four feet. He looked around the hallways. There were lots of animals hanging around. Like Salem, all of the students at the O.R. Obedience Boarding School had once been witches or warlocks. But they had been sentenced by the Witches' Council to years as familiars for committing various crimes. Now they were at obedience school for doing even more bad things.

The familiars at the school weren't all cats, though. Some were reptiles, some were dogs, some were snakes, some were birds, and some were rodents. *Boy, those guys must have done something* really *evil,* Salem thought to himself as he stared at a group of little gray mice.

Salem walked down the hallway until he found his locker—number 1313 (talk about bad luck!). He used his teeth to turn the combination lock and opened the locker.

"Phew! The last person who used this locker must have kept a full supply of smelly gym socks and egg salad sandwiches in here!" Salem exclaimed as the stink from his new locker filled the hallway.

"Talking to yourself, feline freak?" a bright red chameleon asked Salem sarcastically.

"Huh?" Salem was taken by surprise. "Uh, hi. I'm Salem. I'm new around here."

"No kidding," the chameleon replied. "I know who you are. I know *everything*

33

that goes on here. After all, I am the head cheerleader."

Wow! Salem thought. *I'm just here a few minutes and already the head cheerleader is flirting with me.*

"So what's your name, gorgeous?" Salem asked in his most debonair voice.

"That doesn't matter to you, cat." The cheerleading chameleon looked at Salem with disgust. "I'm just here to make sure you know your place. And in this school, cats are at the bottom of the food chain. Even mice are cooler than cats."

Before Salem could reply, a whole crowd of chameleons gathered in the hall. They circled around the head cheerleader.

"Oooh. Tibby. You're all red. I just love that color on you!" a yellow chameleon exclaimed. She moved a little closer to Tibby. Instantly, the yellow chameleon turned red.

"I adore red!" A blue chameleon shouted through the hall. She moved closer to Tibby as well. Suddenly the blue chameleon turned red.

One by one the chameleon cheerleading squad members changed their skin tone to bright red. As they all walked away, giggling among themselves, Salem breathed a sigh of relief. At least that was over.

But not for long.

Salem felt someone's hot breath on his neck. He turned slowly and came face to chest with the largest, meanest looking, greyhound racing dog he'd ever seen.

"He-he-hello," Salem stammered nervously. "I'm S-s-s-alem."

"I don't care what your name is!" the greyhound barked at Salem. He bared his sharp fangs. "But you'd better remember mine. I'm Rodney. And if I ever see you talking to—or even looking at—my girl-

friend Tibby again, I'll tear you into pieces."

"Okay," Salem said quickly. "I'll stay as far from Tibby as possible." *With pleasure.*

"You'd better . . . *Cat!*" Rodney ordered. "And stay away from me and the rest of the track team, too. We athletes don't like cats. Cats are really dumb."

Suddenly, an unfamiliar voice interrupted Rodney. "Actually, cats are far more intelligent than dogs. In fact studies show that . . ."

Salem was shocked to discover that someone was sticking up for him. He looked gratefully at a small gray tabby cat with green eyes and horn-rimmed glasses who had stepped between Rodney and Salem and was at that very moment spewing off facts about the intelligence of felines.

"Oh man! *Two* cats!" Rodney declared.

"I've gotta get out of here. I don't want people to think I just moved to Loserville!"

As Rodney ran off, Salem showed his gratitude to the tabby. "Thanks!" he said. "I'm happy to see another feline face around here. I'm Salem."

"I'm Smitty," the other cat replied. "It's nice to meet someone who is bound to be as unpopular around here as I am."

Salem felt his back arch. *Unpopular!* Salem Saberhagen had never been unpopular in his entire life. Why even back when he was trying to become a warlock dictator in charge of the whole world, people loved him—or they were at least afraid to tell him otherwise.

"I'm not unpopular," Salem told Smitty.

"Whatever you say," Smitty said. "Anyway I've got to go. I'm late for class."

As Smitty walked down the hall, Salem sighed. This school thing wasn't going too well so far. Still, there was a chance

37

that he would make some new friends once he started his classes.

Salem looked down at his schedule. His first class was English. *That's good. I already speak that,* he thought as he walked down the hall, searching for Room 101. Salem was so busy looking at the room numbers on the classroom doors that he walked right into a tall, bony, middle-aged woman who was carrying a laptop computer in her arms. A small, fluffy dog who looked like a mop with eyes stood by her side.

"Aaah!" the woman cried out. "There's something furry on my foot!"

"Sorry," Salem apologized. "I was just looking for my class."

"Oh no, not another cat. I can't stand cats!" the woman exclaimed.

"I've been hearing a lot of that lately," Salem murmured.

"What did you say?"

"Forget it. Now if you'll just get out of my way, I have to get to English class," Salem replied.

"Do you know who I am?" the woman bellowed.

"No," Salem answered. "But I'll bet you're going to tell me."

The little dog growled at Salem. Salem hissed at the dog.

"I am Miss Stake, the vice principal of this school, and this," she pointed to the dog, "is Fluffy. He's my dog, *and* my best friend."

Salem shook his head. Things were going from bad to worse. The vice principal was a dog lover!

Miss Stake pushed a button on her computer. "What did you say your name was again?" she asked.

"I didn't say," Salem said.

"Oh, a wise guy, eh? Well, what *is* your name?"

"Salem Saberhagen."

Miss Stake typed Salem's name into the computer. "A prankster, eh? Well there won't be any pranking around here, Mr. Saberhagen. Fluffy and I will be keeping an eye on you. And the next time you are in the halls after the bell rings, you had better have a pass!"

Chapter 6

Salem finally made his way to his English class. He slid into a seat behind a group of snakes and waited for the teacher to begin.

The teacher was a middle-aged warlock with a pot belly and a long bushy moustache. Salem thought he saw part of the teacher's breakfast still stuck in the hairs of his moustache. *Yuck!*

"Class, my name is Mr. Watto. Welcome to English for Familiars. Here's your first

41

question. Which response is correct to the introduction I just made? 'Hello Mr. Watto' or 'How ya doin' teach'?"

Salem was happy. Obviously this class was going to be a breeze. But as he looked around the room, he noticed that none of his classmates were raising their paws, wings, or rattlesnake tails to answer the question.

Man, what a bunch of losers, Salem thought. *This is such an easy one.* Salem raised his paw high. Mr. Watto nodded in his direction.

"Hello Mr. Watto," Salem replied.

"Wrong!" Mr. Watto bellowed.

Salem nearly fell out of his seat. "What do you mean, I'm wrong?"

Mr. Watto shot Salem an evil stare. "There *is* no proper response," Mr. Watto informed Salem. "Familiars are meant to be seen and not heard when they are in the company of witches, warlocks, or humans. It seems you are in the correct place Mr. Saberhagen—you need to learn obedience!"

When his English class was finally over, Salem looked at his schedule. His next class was a flower arranging seminar. That was not exactly Salem's idea of fun, especially when the teacher told the class that, "Making pretty floral arrangements for your witches' homes will keep them happy. And keeping his mistress happy is the job of any good familiar."

Salem's goal had never exactly been to keep Zelda, Hilda, or Sabrina happy. In fact, he liked to think that in some ways, *he* ran the Spellman household. It was all that was left of his once-great empire. In Salem's mind, he wasn't the Spellmans' pet, *they* were his people.

I'm not going to let this place break me! Salem vowed as he walked through the

crowded halls after having spent a full hour arranging a vase of roses and daffodils. Making his way down the hallway was no easy task. Salem had to avoid the pack of greyhounds who were practicing for their track meet by jumping over their classmates as though they were hurdles.

From the corner of his eye, Salem spotted Fluffy standing right outside Miss Stake's office door. Fluffy's eyes closed to little angry slits as he stared at Salem. Fluffy was carrying something yellow in his mouth, but Salem was too far away to see what the dog was holding.

Just then, Miss Stake walked out of her office. She was looking at her laptop computer screen and not watching where she was going. Just as Miss Stake took a step toward Salem, Fluffy dropped the yellow item in front of her. It was a banana peel.

"Yikes!" Miss Stake cried out as she

slipped on the peel and landed flat on her back.

Salem knew he shouldn't laugh, but he couldn't help himself. That was one good practical joke—even if it was performed by a dog.

But the joke was on Salem.

First, everyone in the hall went completely silent. Then they all stared right at Salem.

"What?" Salem asked them. "Come on. That was a good one."

But Fluffy ignored Salem. Instead, the small pooch ran right up to Miss Stake, licked her on the arm, and tried to comfort her.

"Fluffy, who did this?" Miss Stake demanded.

There was a gleam of joy in Fluffy's face as he pointed his paw directly toward Salem.

Salem tried to run. But Miss Stake had

45

already spotted him. "Salem Saberhagen!" she shouted. "You are going to be sorry!"

"But it wasn't me. I didn't do it. It was him," Salem cried out, pointing toward Fluffy.

Fluffy looked up at Miss Stake with falsely innocent eyes.

"Now you're lying too," Miss Stake charged Salem. "And you are accusing my darling Fluffy of hurting me. This is totally unacceptable."

Miss Stake stood up and picked up her computer. "Oh dear!" she moaned. "The delete button was pressed when I hit the ground. My whole morning schedule has been erased! Where will I go? What will I do?"

Quickly, the flustered vice principal returned to her office, with Fluffy at her heels. Just before the dog entered the office, he turned and stuck out his pink tongue at Salem.

46

A moment later, an announcement came over the loudspeaker.

"Attention all students! This is Miss Stake. A new student, Salem Saberhagen, has decided to be a practical joker. But as we all know, jokes have no place in obedience school. And, since in this school we are all responsible for one another's behavior, I am giving the entire student body extra homework this afternoon! And just to make sure you have time to do the work, all sporting events will be canceled."

Salem gulped. No sporting events! Now the jocks and the cheerleaders would *really* be on his case. And so would everybody else.

This was going to be a long three weeks.

Chapter 7

Salem was definitely the B.L.O.C. (Big Loser on Campus). Everyone hated him, and they weren't afraid to let him know it.

One afternoon Salem made the mistake of standing within ten feet of Tibby, the cheerleading chameleon, and looking in her direction. It was hard *not* to look at Tibby. She was standing near a bright yellow bulletin board, and her skin had changed color to match the board. One by one the other cheerleading chameleons gathered around her, each changing their skin color until, once again, all the cheerleaders had skin the same color as Tibby's. They looked like a big bunch of bananas.

Before Salem ever knew what hit him, two members of the snake wrestling team wrapped themselves around Salem and held him still. Salem screeched as Rodney picked him up with his teeth, and shoved him into locker 1313.

"That'll teach you to look at my girlfriend!" Rodney shouted at Salem as he slammed the locker door shut.

"That's where freaks belong," Salem heard Tibby say as she and Rodney walked off. "Locked away."

As Salem sat alone in the dark, smelly, locker, he heard the jocks and cheerleaders laughing at him. He pushed on the door, but it seemed that Rodney had locked it.

49

"Help! Help! Sabrina, Zelda, Hilda, anybody! Help!"

But Salem knew deep down that screaming for Sabrina and her aunts wasn't going to help him now. They couldn't hear him, and even if they could, they wouldn't be able to help him. The Witches' Council would never approve of them interfering with a punishment. Salem was going to be stuck in this smelly locker for the next three weeks, all alone and hungry.

Suddenly there was a flash of light, as the locker door popped open. Salem blinked and looked up to see Smitty standing in front of him. The tabby was holding a small hairpin in his teeth.

"Thanks. How did you manage to open the locker?" Salem asked.

"I picked the lock," Smitty replied simply.

Salem looked impressed.

"Did I mention that I was a jewel thief when I was a warlock?" Smitty asked Salem, as he helped the black cat out from the locker. "That's what got me turned into a cat in the first place."

Salem shook his head. "I think I would have remembered if the word 'jewel' had entered the conversation. The only thing you mentioned to me was that you were unpopular."

"*We're* unpopular," Smitty corrected him.

"Whatever." Salem sighed. There was no point arguing about it now.

"You know, you probably wouldn't have gotten into so much trouble if you hadn't messed up Miss Stake's computer system," Smitty explained. "She lives by that thing. All of her schedules are in there, and so are the names of all the students. She can't go five minutes without

checking her computer. It's the only way she knows when classes are over or when the next athletic meet is supposed to begin. Sometimes I think the computer even tells her when to go to the bathroom."

Salem laughed at that. Then he got serious. "*I* didn't mess it up, though," Salem explained. "Fluffy did."

"Oh, she'd never believe that," Smitty said. "Even though it's true. Miss Stake would never do anything to Fluffy. Fluffy is Miss Stake's only friend. And that's pretty amazing, considering even *he* hates her!"

Salem was amazed. Smitty seemed to know everything that was going on at the school.

"Well, I've gotta be off," Smitty told Salem. "There's a book I want to pick up at the library. Do you want to come along?"

Salem shook his head. "No. I'm actually kind of hungry. I'm going to go grab a snack in the cafeteria."

"Suit yourself," Smitty answered with a shrug, leaving Salem alone in the hall.

Chapter 8

The cafeteria was buzzing with the sounds of students who were free—at least for a little while—of the rules and regulations of the classrooms. It was the one place in the O.R. Obedience Boarding School where the students didn't have to be, well, obedient.

The cheerleaders were sitting at one end of a long table. The athletes were sitting at the table behind them. Other students were sitting at various tables around the room, eating the gray slop that was served day after day in the cafeteria and talking about all of the things that were going on in the school.

But as soon as Salem walked into the cafeteria, the room went silent. Everyone just stared as he got into line for his bowl of slop. A flock of birds who were ahead of Salem in line flew out of the way and let him go first. They didn't want to be seen with him for even a minute.

Salem used his nose to push his bowl of slop over to the far end of a table that was filled with cats. The other cats jumped up and raced to the other side of the room.

Great. Now even the other cats don't want to sit with me. Life would be easier if the Witches' Council had turned me into a dog. Salem jumped. *A dog!* What was he thinking?

This place is really getting to me!

Salem sat alone at the table and began to slowly lick at his bowl of gray, slimy food. After a while, a voice interrupted his thoughts. "Do you mind if I sit here?"

It was Smitty. Salem was relieved. At least he wouldn't have to eat alone. "Sure. If you want to."

Smitty took a seat next to Salem on the long bench.

"I thought you were going to the library."

Smitty nodded. "I just needed to check something out for my history class. I had to read a chapter in a book about manners during the time of King Henry the Eighth."

Salem started laughing.

"What's so funny?" Smitty asked him.

"That's the first time I ever heard the words 'manners' and 'Henry the Eighth' in the same sentence."

Smitty looked confused.

"I knew Henry the Eighth," Salem explained. "And his idea of manners was to chomp on a giant turkey leg and then talk with his mouth full!"

"You knew King Henry the Eighth?" Smitty exclaimed. "Wow!"

Salem sat up regally in his seat. "Oh yes. Before the Witches' Council turned me into a cat, I knew a lot of royals. Cleopatra had a real thing for me!"

Smitty was impressed. "Really?"

Salem nodded, but he didn't actually reply. The truth was, Cleopatra had once broken a date with Salem so she could go out on the town with Julius Caesar, but Smitty didn't have to know *all* the details, did he?

Salem looked curiously at Smitty. The guy seemed so smart and well-behaved. He studied. He went to classes. And he never bothered anyone. Salem couldn't

57

imagine what a cat like Smitty would be doing in obedience school.

"How come you're here?" Salem asked him finally.

"I used a computer to steal millions of dollars from banks," Smitty explained. "I transferred the money into a Swiss bank account in my name. I figured once my sentence as a cat was over and I became a warlock again, I could use the cash."

Now it was Salem's turn to be impressed. Salem loved anything that had to do with large sums of money. "You'll have to show me how to do that sometime," Salem told Smitty. "Being put in here for a while doesn't seem like too bad a punishment for getting all that cash."

Smitty shook his head. "I had to give the money back. And I'm stuck here for a year!"

Salem nodded with understanding. "Oh, that *is* bad!"

"So what are you in for, Salem?"

Salem sat low in his seat. After hearing what Smitty had done, Salem's crimes didn't seem so impressive. "I made a few phony phone calls," he replied, waiting for Smitty to laugh.

But Smitty didn't laugh. In fact, he seemed impressed. "What kind of calls did you make?"

Salem told Smitty about his refrigerator joke and about the snew. Then he told him about the rubber rat he'd put in the freezer and how the fake spider had scared Willard Kraft half to death. The two cats had a good laugh over Salem's pranks.

"Those were the good old days," Salem said finally. "I really miss home."

"Me, too," Smitty said. "And I still have eight months left here. I sure wish there was a way to escape."

Salem looked at his new friend.

59

Suddenly a plan began hatching in his furry little head.

"You know, with your computer know-how, and my brains and amazing creativity, we just *might* be able to break out of this place," Salem told Smitty.

"If we get caught, we could be stuck here for a really long time," Smitty reminded Salem nervously.

Salem sniffed at the horrible gray slop in his bowl. He thought of the yummy tuna he had stashed away under Sabrina's bed. He remembered the soft new pink wool sweater Sabrina had just bought—just perfect for unraveling. Salem just had to get home.

"I think it's worth the risk."

Chapter 9

That night, after everyone was asleep, Salem and Smitty snuck out of their rooms. They met in the hallway outside of Miss Stake's office. It was time to put Salem's plan into action.

Smitty used his talents to unlock the doors to the janitor's closet, the gym, the cafeteria, and Miss Stake's office. Then the two cats gathered their supplies and got to work.

"By the time we're through with this

place, nothing will ever be the same," Salem whispered to Smitty. "And while everybody is trying to figure out how to fix things and get them back to normal, you and I will be able to just slip out the front door to freedom."

"I hope you're right," Smitty replied in a hushed voice. "Because if you're not, we're really in for it."

"Oh it will work," Salem promised as he padded off toward the cafeteria, dragging a bucket of paint behind him. "It has to."

The next morning, the students at the O.R. Obedience Boarding School awoke to a frantic announcement by Miss Stake.

"Everybody get up right away. And hurry to class. Someone has turned off all of the bells in the school, and reset the time. I don't care what the clocks say, it is now eight forty-five. Classes begin in fifteen minutes. Anyone who is late will be given detention!"

The students raced out of bed, got ready, and ran through the halls to class.

Suddenly, Miss Stake emerged from her office. She was wearing a pair of running pants and a sweatshirt. Fluffy ran by her side as the vice principal darted down the hall.

Suddenly she was stopped by a woman in a dark gray suit. "Miss Stake, where are you going?" the woman asked.

"I'm covering for the gym teacher today at nine o'clock," Miss Stake said. "Why are you here, Mrs. Stepon?"

"I'm here for the Other Realm Board of Education meeting," Mrs. Stepon replied. "It's a very important meeting, and you are scheduled to speak. Don't you remember?"

Miss Stake opened her ever-present laptop computer. "But it says right here

that I am supposed to be in the gym," Miss Stake said. She pointed to the computer. But instead of Miss Stake's schedule, there was a chat room of teenagers who were debating a very serious question—who was better, the Backstreet Boys or 'N Sync.

"Someone has been messing around with my computer!" Miss Stake bellowed through the hall.

Mrs. Stepon flinched. "Miss Stake! That kind of behavior is not suitable for an obedience school!"

Miss Stake flushed. "I'm very sorry. Just give me two minutes to change, and I'll be right with you."

Suddenly the computer beeped. It was one of Miss Stake's warning signals. Miss Stake pushed a button and turned the computer off. "I do not have to go the bathroom just yet!" she declared.

"I knew it!" Smitty whispered to Salem

as the two cats hid behind a row of lockers. "That thing really does tell her when to go!"

The plan was in motion. Salem raised his paw and gave Smitty a high five.

"Who did this!" Rodney's voice suddenly rang out from the gym.

Throngs of students raced over to see what had happened. Salem and Smitty joined the crowd. But the two scheming cats weren't the least bit curious about why Rodney was so upset. They knew exactly what had happened in the gym.

"Just look at this! *Look* at this!" Rodney shouted, as he pointed to a long wooden beam. "Someone has been using our balance beam as a scratching post!"

The crowd moved closer. Sure enough, there were literally hundreds of tiny little claw marks running up and down the sides of the balance beam.

"It's ruined! It's absolutely ruined!" Rodney said, as he sat by the beam and ran his paw over the damaged wood. "And that's not the worst of it. Look at the basketball hoops! And the volleyball net."

As the crowd glanced up, Salem tried hard not to snicker. All of the basketball and volleyball nets had been unraveled. He and Smitty had had a great time doing that. It had been almost as much fun as unraveling the yarn in one of Sabrina's sweaters.

"This is awful! Just awful!" Rodney shouted. Then he put his head in his paws and began to cry.

Everyone in the gym became silent. Salem looked over at Tibby. Would she run over and comfort her sad boyfriend?

Yeah, right.

"Oh, how embarrassing!" she moaned. "I hate men who cry. Come on cheerleaders. Let's get out of here before I lose the desire to wave my pom-poms for that loser."

Tibby left the room. Her squad of cheerleaders trailed behind her. As Salem and Smitty saw Tibby heading into the cafeteria, the two cats gave each other a knowing wink.

From the minute Tibby and her group of followers entered the cafeteria, they were in trouble. During the night, Salem had painted the walls a rainbow of colors. That meant that no matter where Tibby sat, her skin began to change its hue. Tibby sat down at a red table that was next to a blue wall. Instantly, her skin changed from red to blue, before finally settling on an extremely unflattering purple. And when she moved to a beige-colored bench near a green wall, her purple skin took on an awful olive green hue.

The other cheerleaders were panicking.

They were having difficulty keeping up with Tibby's never-ending color changes. It was becoming almost impossible for them to all look exactly the same.

"This is horrible," Tibby announced as she ran away from the green and beige and wound up standing next to a red-and-white striped window shade. Almost instantly her skin took on the exact same pattern. "I look awful in stripes."

As a squad, the cheerleaders now looked like a giant chameleon hodgepodge. Their skin was all blotchy with spots of red, white, purple, beige, green, and orange. Now, instead of looking chameleon cool, they looked like chameleon clowns!

"My skin is getting very tired. How am I supposed to win the homecoming queen contest with tired skin?" Tibby cried out.

A crowd of familiars had gathered in the cafeteria. They were all staring at the cheerleaders and laughing. Now that was a switch!

Salem was very pleased with the way things were going. The once-organized vice principal was now a total mess as her computer kept sending her to the wrong place at the wrong time. The tough greyhound track stars had become a group of whimpering pups, crying over their athletic equipment. And the once too-cool cheerleaders were now the laughingstock of the school. Everything at the O.R. Obedience Boarding School was completely out of control!

It was time to put the finishing touches on Salem's plan. He and Smitty quickly raced toward the main office. "Are you sure Miss Stake isn't there?" Salem asked Smitty.

Smitty looked at his watch. "Right about now, her computer should be telling her to go show the cooking class how to

make a pineapple upside-down cake," Smitty assured Salem. "And since she always does what her computer tells her to, she'll be nowhere near the office."

That was all Salem needed to hear. He ran into the room and leaped up on the counter. Then he used his paw to turn on the school address system.

"Fellow students! Are you sick of eating gray slop in the cafeteria? I know I am! I want caviar! I want salmon! I want cream! *No more slop! No more slop!*"

Salem turned off the public-address system and listened to find out whether or not his message had gotten through. From the hallway he could hear other students picking up his chant.

"No more slop! No more slop!" the animals in the hall shouted. "No Meat! No Peace!"

The protest march made its way to the cafeteria. Salem and Smitty followed the marchers through the double doors.

Splat! Salem had to duck as a big bowl of gooey gray slop flew just over his head and landed on the wall.

"Food fight!" one of the dogs shouted as he heaved a huge tray of slop across the cafeteria.

Before long, there was gray slop all over the walls of the cafeteria. The cheerleaders started crying as their skin turned the color of slop. The greyhounds tried to run through the cafeteria to help the chameleons, but they kept slipping on the slimy stuff.

There was no sign of obedience anywhere.

"This is it Smitty," Salem shouted to his friend. "Let's make a run for it!"

Chapter 10

Sabrina was in her room when she heard the scratching on the linen closet door. That could only mean one thing—a visitor from the Other Realm. She ran out into the hall to find out who it was.

"Salem!" Sabrina shouted with surprise as she opened the door to the linen closet. "What are you doing back so soon?"

Salem leaped into Sabrina's arms.

"Hide me!" he begged her. "They're going to come for me, I know it!"

"*Who* is going to come for you? What are you talking about?"

"Just take me in your room and lock the door," Salem said. "Oh, and get me a can of tuna, okay? I'm starved."

Sabrina scowled. "It doesn't seem like you got very obedient at that school."

Salem sighed. "Okay. *Please.*"

"That's better. Go hide under my bed. I'll be back with the food in a minute."

Salem grimaced. "Are you kidding? You've got stuff *growing* under that bed. I'll just curl up in your covers."

Now it was Sabrina's turn to be disgusted. "Oh great. It's back to sleeping with fur balls," she muttered as she went downstairs to the kitchen.

A few minutes later, Sabrina returned with the eats. "Okay, now fill me in," she asked Salem.

73

Salem quickly swallowed a few bites of tuna, and let out a small belch.

"Boy, that must've been some obedience school," Sabrina teased. "Look at all the lovely things you learned there."

"Excuse me," Salem apologized. "Look, the only thing I learned in that school was that I'm glad I'm not a chameleon."

Sabrina looked confused. "Huh?"

Salem began to tell Sabrina all about what went on at the school. He told her about the cheerleading chameleons, the track-running greyhounds, and Miss Stake. He finished the story by telling her how he and Smitty had finally escaped.

"Wow!" Sabrina exclaimed when Salem was through. "I always wondered what it would be like to go to high school in the Other Realm. Now I know. It isn't any different there than it is here.

And at least here, I have my boyfriend, Harvey."

"Is that a good thing or a bad thing?" Salem snickered.

Sabrina frowned. "Hey! Do you want me to hide you or what?" she demanded.

Salem thought about the life he had just left. "Sorry," he apologized quickly. "I'll do anything you want. Just don't make me go back to that school!"

"Well, you can't hide here forever," Sabrina told Salem finally. "I mean sooner or later things at the school are going to settle down, and they are going to realize that you are missing. Then someone will come looking for you."

Just then, Sabrina heard a knock at the linen closet door. She ran out of her room and went to the closet.

As she opened the door, a tall bony woman barged through. The woman

barely looked at Sabrina as she typed furiously on her portable keyboard.

"Uh, Salem," Sabrina called as she shut the linen closet door behind Miss Stake. "I think it's going to be sooner, rather than later."

Chapter 11

Sabrina held tight to Salem as she led Miss Stake to the living room. Sabrina may have been angry at the cat before, but she didn't want him to have to go back to that horrible school.

"I'll get you a cup of tea," Sabrina hurriedly told the vice principal. She ran into the kitchen, with Salem in tow.

Quickly, Sabrina popped a note into the toaster and waited for it to be sent by special messenger to the Other Realm. In

77

an instant, her two aunts popped into the kitchen. They were dressed in white robes. Their faces were covered in green goo.

"Nice look," Salem told the sisters. "Slime time."

"Very funny," Hilda said. "We were in the middle of getting facials on Mars. It's supposed to make you look a hundred years younger."

"Salem, what are you doing here?" Zelda asked. "You are supposed to be in obedience school for at least two more weeks."

"There's a slight problem with that," Sabrina began slowly. Then she quickly filled her aunts in on Salem's dilemma.

Once Sabrina had finished talking, Zelda shook her head. "I feel bad for you Salem, I really do," she said slowly. "But when the Witches' Council lays down the law, it can't be changed. And the judge said that you are required to go to obedience school for three weeks. Nobody ever led you to believe that it was going to be a picnic. After all, it was a punishment."

Zelda took Salem from Sabrina's arms and carried him into the living room. She reached out and tried to hand the cat over to Miss Stake. "I think this is who you're looking for," Zelda told the vice principal.

But to everyone's surprise, Miss Stake jumped away from Zelda's reach. "Get that cat away!" she shouted. "I don't want him anywhere near me."

Zelda looked surprised. "But didn't you come here to take Salem back to school?"

"Are you crazy?" Miss Stake replied. "I'll be a whole lot happier if I never see that cat again. You wouldn't believe the mess he made of my school. It will

take our cheerleaders years to get their complexions back! And I'm going to have to hire a world-class chef for the cafeteria. Frankly, I think Salem should be kept as far from our school as possible!"

"Are you going to call the Witches' Council and report him?" Sabrina asked nervously.

Miss Stake shook her head. "I'd rather they not find out about this whole incident. As it is, I have the school board on my case for missing a very important meeting—thanks to Salem and his little friend Smitty."

"But he still has two weeks on his obedience school sentence," Hilda reminded the vice principal. "The Witches' Council is going to demand that he finish that."

"I know," Miss Stake replied. "And I fully intend to see that he passes all of his courses. Just not at my school. In fact, I have a plan that should keep everybody involved satisfied and happy. Everyone except for Mr. Saberhagen, of course."

"Of course," Salem moaned.

Chapter 12

Salem, Salem, big and able, get your furry paws off the table," Sabrina sang.

Instantly, Salem leaped off the table and onto the kitchen floor.

"Nicely done," Sabrina told the cat. "Now go over and eat your lunch. And try not to spill any this time."

Salem padded his way over to his bowl. He looked at the food and scowled. "Canned cat food again?" he asked her. "When am I going to get something good, like salmon coquettes? I love those."

"Now Salem, you know it's not obedient to question the menu," Sabrina said. She looked down at the schedule she carried with her on a clipboard. "After lunch, we have to do some more work on your composition about *How I Can Better Serve My Owners*. I don't think writing 'My owners should serve *me*' is quite what Miss Stake had in mind when she assigned it to you. And besides, the essay is supposed to be five *hundred* words, not five!"

Salem shook his head. "Have you ever tried to write five hundred words holding the pencil in your teeth?" Salem demanded. "Look Sabrina, don't you think you're taking this home-schooling thing a bit too hard? I mean, just because Miss Stake named you as my teacher, doesn't mean that you—"

83

Sabrina shook her head. "Salem, it's not polite to talk with your mouth full."

Salem let out a little moan. He almost wished he hadn't pulled so many practical jokes on Sabrina over the past few months. Now she was getting back at him for the pencil circle on her yearbook photo, as well as for every time he'd short-sheeted her bed or ordered a pizza with extra anchovies in her name—and made her pay for it.

Granted, being allowed to finish out his school term at home with Sabrina as his teacher was better than going back to the Other Realm Obedience Boarding School. But not by much. Sabrina was as tough as any teacher in the school. And the canned food she fed Salem was barely a step up from the slop in the cafeteria. And there was no Smitty for him to commiserate with. Salem had tried e-mailing his new pal once or twice, only to discover that the Witches' Council had cut off his computer access for the next four hundred years.

"Salem, finish up your lunch," Sabrina ordered the cat. "You have a lot to do. After you work on your essay, you still have to reknit my lavender sweater that you unraveled. At the rate you're going, by the time you finish, my sweater will be out of style."

Salem buried his head in his paws. He couldn't wait for the next two weeks to end. There was no doubt about it. Having Sabrina Spellman for a teacher was no joke!

Cat Care Tips

1. Scratching objects such as furniture comes naturally to cats, and you can't completely prevent your cat from scratching. However, if your cat scratches your furniture and carpet, you should provide it with an alternative place to scratch, such as a scratching post or a piece of old carpet, where your cat spends most of its time.

2. If your cat doesn't like to use its scratching post, try different kinds. Some cats prefer a specific type—wood, cardboard, or carpeted posts are the most common. Your cat may have a preference.

3. You can also train your cat to use its scratching post by gently showing it how and giving it praise or treats when it uses the post instead of your furniture. (Sprinkling catnip on the post may help your cat make a positive association with the scratching area.) Remember, the earlier you start to train your kitty not to scratch furniture, the better it will learn!

Sabrina
The Teenage Witch®

Salem's Tails™

What's it like to be a powerful warlock,
sentenced to one hundred years in a
cat's body for trying to take over the world?
Ask Salem.

**Read all about Salem's magical
adventures in this series based on the hit
ABC-TV show!**

Look for a new title every other month

A MINSTREL® BOOK
Published by Pocket Books

2007-10